2·19·17

To: Sadé
From: Mommy

© SAGOSKATT
The Friends in Fantasy Forest
Project manager: Lena Allblom, IKEA of Sweden AB
Project coordinator: Anders Truedsson, TITEL Books AB
Text: Ulf Stark
Illustrations: Sara Nilsson Bergman
Typesetting: Gyllene Snittet AB, Sweden
Translation: Comactiva Language Partner AB, Sweden
Produced by IKEA of Sweden AB
Paper: Arcoset FSC
Printing: Litopat S.p.A., Italy 2015
TITEL Books AB for IKEA of Sweden AB. All rights reserved.

We aim to provide as much inspiration as possible, but with minimal impact on the environment. All our books take the environment into account in every stage of production, from the choice of paper to how we distribute our printed material.

The book you are holding is printed on paper that meets all the requirements for responsible forestry. This means, for example, that the paper raw material comes from trees that are certified to originate from a sustainably managed forest. We print using vegetable-based printing inks without solvents, and the printers are located close to our large markets to avoid long-distance transport to you.

We are also working to develop the printed medium so that it minimises impact on the environment in the future. Read more about our environmental work at www.ikea.co.uk

FSC
www.fsc.org
MIX
Paper from responsible sources
FSC® C018744

The Friends in Fantasy Forest

Ulf Stark

Sara Nilsson Bergman

"Welcome to my place!" is what it says on the door to Tuka's home.

Tuka lives in Fantasy Forest with all the other fantasy animals. Today he is happy. That's because his best friend Kota is coming to visit. And tomorrow, yes tomorrow, is his BIRTHDAY!

He has just poured two glasses of squash when Kota arrives.

"Come outside," says Kota. "It's been snowing. We can slide down the hill."

"Let's have a glass of squash first," says Tuka. "Tomorrow we can drink with straws, because it's my birthday."

"Oh, your birthday?" says Kota. "What do you do on a birthday?"

"You give presents," says Tuka. "To me, because it's *my* day."

"What kind of presents?"

"The one who is giving the present decides what to give. But it has to be something nice that I will be happy to get."

Kota goes quiet because he is thinking about what Tuka likes best of all.

What a beautiful day it is today!

The snow is sparkling. And even though it's snowing the trees are full of fruit: swirlipops, bringles, plombles and ripe yellow squarges. If you get hungry you can just pick some, because that's the way it is in Fantasy Forest. It can be winter and summer at the same time, and autumn and spring in fact.

Tuka and Kota each pick a big swirlipop leaf. They are big and smooth, and they have a useful handle to hold when you're sliding down a hill.

"This one fits my bottom perfectly," says Tuka.

"Yay, let's get sliding!" says Kota.

So they go to the hill where all the others are.

Nora with the big ears is there.

So is Beli with the hat, and Cany who has a horn on his nose. And Cypro with the long neck and the long, pink body like a dress.

She is the first one to see Tuka and Kota.

"They're here!" she cries.

"Hooray, it's Tuka and Kota!" says Malaya and claps her green hands. "Hi there, let's play!"

"No, let's have a competition! I want us to have a competition!" howls Teeva.

She jumps up and down making big snow puffs with her yellow paws. Teeva always wants to have a competition. That's the kind of animal she is.

"Well *I'm* not competing," says Romi and spreads her black wings. "I'm going to make air shapes."

"And I want to shake hands with the new arrivals," says Nel.

This takes a while, because Nel likes to shake all six of his hands.

After that, it is time for the competitions.

They race each other down the hill. The first time, Nora wins. She flaps her ears with joy. Teeva comes third.

"Woohoo!" she shouts, jumping up and down and swishing her tail. "Three is my favourite number!"

Next time, Malaya wins. She giggles so much that her sharp teeth sparkle like the snow. Teeva comes eighth. She is absolutely delighted with that.

"Woohoo again!" she cries. "Eight is the most beautiful number there is."

And she draws a figure eight in the snow with her tail to show everyone how beautiful it is.

After that, they have a competition to see who can run *up* the hill the fastest. Beli is the winner. He has such strong green legs. Cany comes second. And Teeva, she comes seventh. She is overjoyed about that.

"This must be my lucky day!" she screams. "Seven, just like the seven days of the week!"

"Well tomorrow it's Tuka's day," says Kota.

"What?" says Nel to Tuka. "Do you have your very own day?"

"Yes," he says. "Tomorrow is my birthday and there's going to be a party."

"We will drink squash with straws," says Kota.

"We'll all come!" cries Beli, and throws his hat in the air where Romi is flying around doing somersaults.

Just then, the wind starts blowing. Cypro extends her neck. She grabs hold of Beli's hat before it gets blown away.

Because that's the way it is in Fantasy Forest: all of a sudden – in no time at all – the wind can start blowing clouds and hats and leaves all over the place. Or it can start raining so all the little leaves go pitter-patter. And then suddenly the sun starts shining and you can swim in the forest lake where all the fantasy fish live.

But right now, it's very windy.

All the animals want to go home to their lovely warm homes.

"See you tomorrow at Tuka's party!" they shout as they all set off in different directions.

The snow is so swirly that it makes Tuka all dizzy.

Luckily, Kota is with him and holds him so he doesn't get blown over.

"What a lovely storm!" says Kota. "Can you hear it howling?"

"I think it's a frightful storm," says Tuka. "And I don't like howling."

He also doesn't like when the trees sway to and fro, sending down great big piles of snow. He wants to get home. It's not a big home, but it's just the right size for him. When he gets home he is going to have something to eat. Then he's going to creep down into his bed and think about TOMORROW. About all the presents he will get. And the party he will organise.

They're nearly there.

And now they are!

BUT WHERE IS THE HOUSE?

"Where is my house?" shrieks Tuka. "It was just here, right by this tree!"

"Hmm, it was right here when I was last here too," says Kota.

"And now it's vanished into thin air!" sobs Tuka. "It's been blown away! My lovely house that had a door you could knock on when you came to visit. How can you come and visit me now? And where am I going to live?"

"You can stay at my house, my dear friend," says Kota.

Isn't it nice of Kota to let Tuka stay at his house? After all, Tuka has nowhere else to go. And it is a delightful house, with curtains on the windows and a sofa with cushions that Tuka can rest his head on.

But it still isn't quite like home.

Kota has served up some breadfruit and herbal tea.

"Go to sleep now," he says. "Tomorrow is *your* day."

"I suppose so," sighs Tuka. "It would be my day if I had a house to have a party in. It would have been a lovely day."

"I'm sure it will all be all right," says Kota. "Night, night."

And off he goes to get into his bed.

But after a while he jumps up again.

"I know!" he cries.

"What do you know?" Tuka wonders.

"Oh, nothing," says Kota. "You go back to sleep, I have to go off and see about something."

And off he goes into the night, where the moon is shining brightly. It is not windy any more. Kota is in a hurry because he has a lot to do.

Tuka is just lying there feeling sorry for himself. "I'm never, ever going to fall asleep," he thinks.

And then he falls asleep.

16

Tuka is woken by someone nudging his tummy.

"Oh Kota!" he cries.

But it's not Kota. It's someone with a horn on their nose. It's Cany.

"Get up," he says, yawning. "You're just lying here sleeping, while we've been up all night working."

"Who's we, and why? And where's Kota?" Tuka wonders.

"I'm afraid he couldn't come. Close your eyes and get on my back. And promise not to look until I say so."

Tuka does as Cany asks. He holds on tight
around Cany's neck, and off they go. He can
smell the fantasy flowers, and hear the fantasy
birds chirping in the fantasy trees. But he still
doesn't feel happy, because he misses his house and his
best friend. A tear squeezes out from under his eye lid
as he thinks about how happy he *should* be.
    Just then, Cany stops.
"You can look now," he says.

And this is what Tuka sees when he opens his eyes:
A HOUSE. With a chimney on the roof, with walls
and windows and a door you can knock on.

In fact, it's a fantasy house. Right by *his* tree.

"I don't believe it!" he cries angrily. "How terribly
rude! Someone, and I don't know who, has built a
house in *my place*! Who on earth is going to live there?"

"You are, dear Tuka," says Cany, beaming with joy. "We
have made it for you! Just open the door and make yourself
at home!"

When Tuka opens the door, he can hardly believe his
eyes. All his friends are standing there: Cypro with the
long neck, Teeva who's not jumping for once, Beli
with his wonky hat, Nora with the tired ears,
Romi who is sitting on Malaya's head,
and of course Nel who is still holding
a hammer, saw, nails and hoof pliers
in his hands.

"Hooray!" they all shout.
"Hooray for Tuka!"

Behind them is a table with ten chairs, and a big cake in the middle. Glasses with straws in. And there are flowers too: red prudelias and yellow systamias. The flowers are cheering too, but very quietly. Everything is exactly the way Tuka imagined it would be on his big day, only much better.

"You lovely, lovely…" he says.

And then he says:

"But how?"

And then:

"And when?"

"During the night," says Beli. "You wouldn't believe how hard we have worked, all night."

"Me most of all," says Nel.

"A new house is quite a good present, isn't it?" says Malaya.

"But where did you get all these things?" Tuka wonders.

"In people's dreams," says Romi. "You wouldn't believe how we had to run around looking in all the dreams of painters and carpenters and metalworkers and bakers."

Because fantasy animals can do that – get inside people's dreams. And sometimes they take things with them.

"It was Kota's idea," says Cypro.

And that's when Tuka notices that Kota isn't there.

"But where is he, my best friend?" he asks. "How can I be happy if he isn't here?"

"He did leave a present for you," says Cany. "Over there!"

He points with his horn to a big box wrapped in nice paper with a ribbon on.

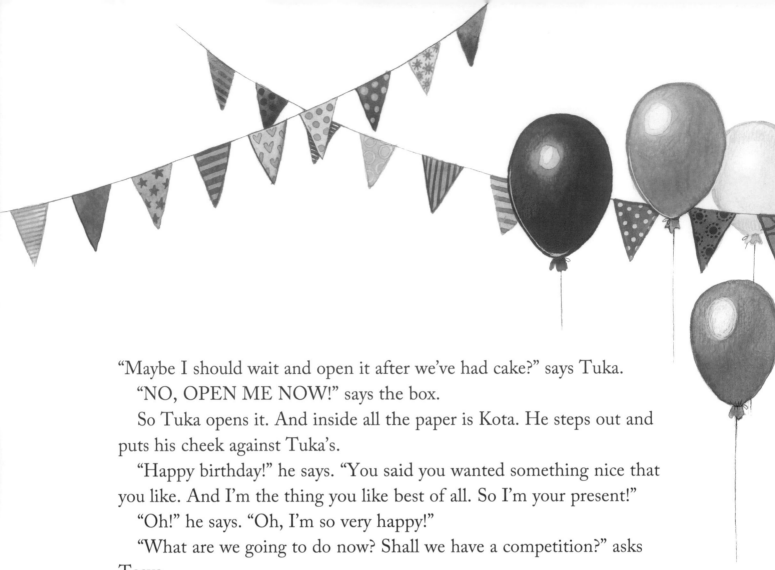

"Maybe I should wait and open it after we've had cake?" says Tuka.

"NO, OPEN ME NOW!" says the box.

So Tuka opens it. And inside all the paper is Kota. He steps out and puts his cheek against Tuka's.

"Happy birthday!" he says. "You said you wanted something nice that you like. And I'm the thing you like best of all. So I'm your present!"

"Oh!" he says. "Oh, I'm so very happy!"

"What are we going to do now? Shall we have a competition?" asks Teeva.

"Yes, let's see who can have the most fun at the party!" says Tuka.

So they do.
And everybody wins!